COPYCAT BEAR!

Ellie Sandall

h
Hodder
Children's
Books

A division of Hachette Children's Books

Mango had a ginormous friend called Blue.

They went
everywhere together.

But there was a problem.
Blue copied **everything**
Mango did.

Mango flapped her wings.
Blue flapped his huge hairy paws.

Mango hopped along the ground.
Blue wobbled from one big paw to the other.

'COPYCAT BEAR!'
said Mango.

Mango flew up into a tree.
'Listen,' she chirped. 'You are a BEAR and I'm a BIRD.
Birds are different from bears. Birds live in trees!

'I do too,' said Blue.

And Blue climbed up
into the tree.

His big arms shook the branches and all the twigs
fell off Mango's new nest.

'Bear brain!' said Mango.
'Now I'm going to sing a song.
But don't copy me! Bears don't sing.'

'Bears do too!' said Blue,
and he took a deep breath...

'RRRI

'COPYCAT BEAR!'

squawked Mango.

'Look! I can fly.
And that is something
bears just don't do!'

'I do!' said Blue
and he jumped...

'OOF!'

…and crashed to the ground,
nearly squashing Mango.

Mango smoothed her tiny feathers and shrilled,

'You see? Bears CAN'T fly.'

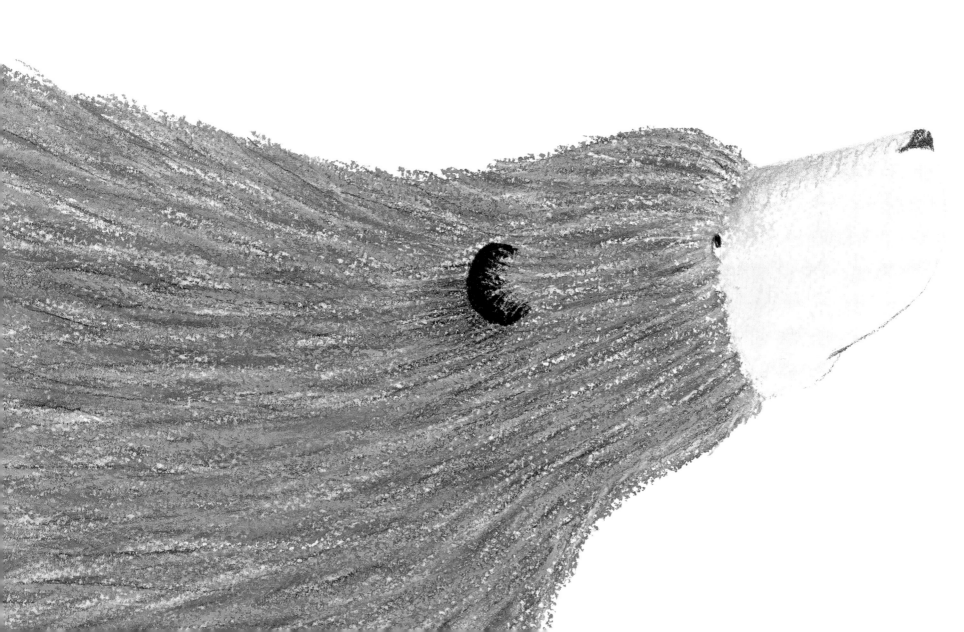

And with that she flew away.

Blue was all alone.

Mango swooped and soared
in the sunlight.

It felt strange to be on her own.
Then she flew down and sat
on a branch.

She started thinking about Blue.

Was he lonely by himself?

Was he thinking about her?

Evening came on and Mango flew off searching
everywhere for Blue.

She found him curled up under the tree where she'd left him.
'Birds are different from bears,' Mango said.
'But they can be best friends.'

She hopped onto his broad back and snuggled into his thick fur.

'I missed you,' she sang softly.

'I missed you too!' said Blue.

'My Copycat Bear,'

said Mango happily.